Dear Parents:

Congratulations! Your child is taking the first steps on an exciting journey. The destination? Independent reading!

STEP INTO READING® will help your child get there. The program offers five steps to reading success. Each step includes fun stories and colorful art or photographs. In addition to original fiction and books with favorite characters, there are Step into Reading Non-Fiction Readers, Phonics Readers and Boxed Sets, Sticker Readers, and Comic Readers—a complete literacy program with something to interest every child.

Learning to Read, Step by Step!

Ready to Read **Preschool–Kindergarten**
• big type and easy words • rhyme and rhythm • picture clues
For children who know the alphabet and are eager to begin reading.

Reading with Help **Preschool–Grade 1**
• basic vocabulary • short sentences • simple stories
For children who recognize familiar words and sound out new words with help.

Reading on Your Own **Grades 1–3**
• engaging characters • easy-to-follow plots • popular topics
For children who are ready to read on their own.

Reading Paragraphs **Grades 2–3**
• challenging vocabulary • short paragraphs • exciting stories
For newly independent readers who read simple sentences with confidence.

Ready for Chapters **Grades 2–4**
• chapters • longer paragraphs • full-color art
For children who want to take the plunge into chapter books but still like colorful pictures.

STEP INTO READING® is designed to give every child a successful reading experience. The grade levels are only guides; children will progress through the steps at their own speed, developing confidence in their reading.

Remember, a lifetime love of reading starts with a single step!

Visit us on the Web!
StepIntoReading.com
rhcbooks.com

Educators and librarians, for a variety of teaching tools, visit us at RHTeachersLibrarians.com

ISBN 978-0-525-57751-5 (trade) — ISBN 978-0-525-57752-2 (lib. bdg.)

Printed in the United States of America 10 9 8 7 6 5 4 3 2 1

Random House Children's Books supports the First Amendment and celebrates the right to read.

STEP INTO READING®

nickelodeon

Save the Rainbow!

by Kristen L. Depken

illustrated by Dave Aikins

Random I

Something is wrong in Zahramay Falls.

A purple mist
touches the genies.
Now they cannot fly!

Leah, Shimmer,
and Shine
follow the mist
to the rainbow falls.
Uh-oh!
There is no purple water.

Princess Samira says
all the colors
in the rainbow falls
have to be there
for genie magic to work.

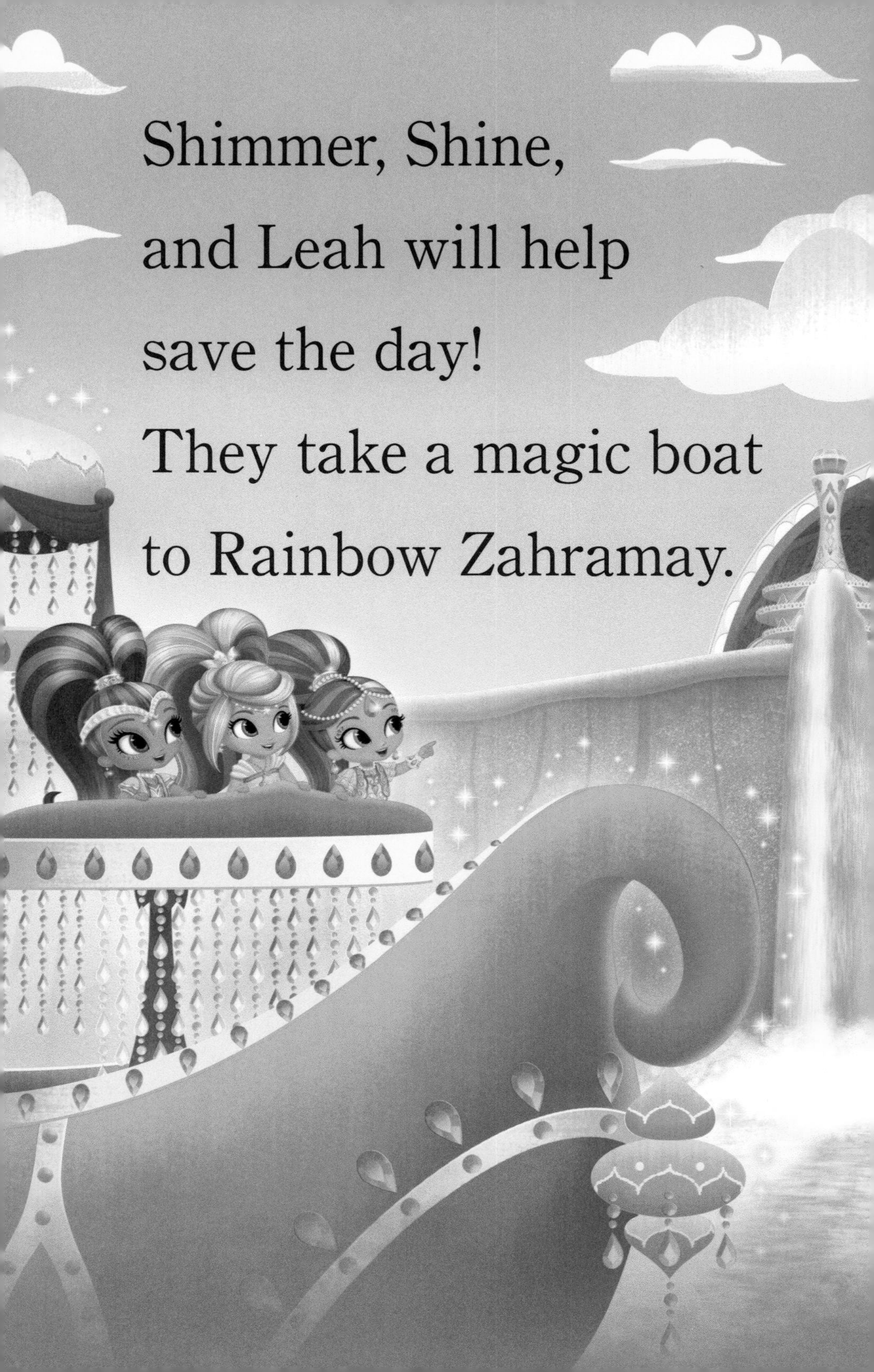

Shimmer, Shine,
and Leah will help
save the day!
They take a magic boat
to Rainbow Zahramay.

They meet Imma,

a rainbow genie.

She can fix

the rainbow falls.

But she needs her staff.

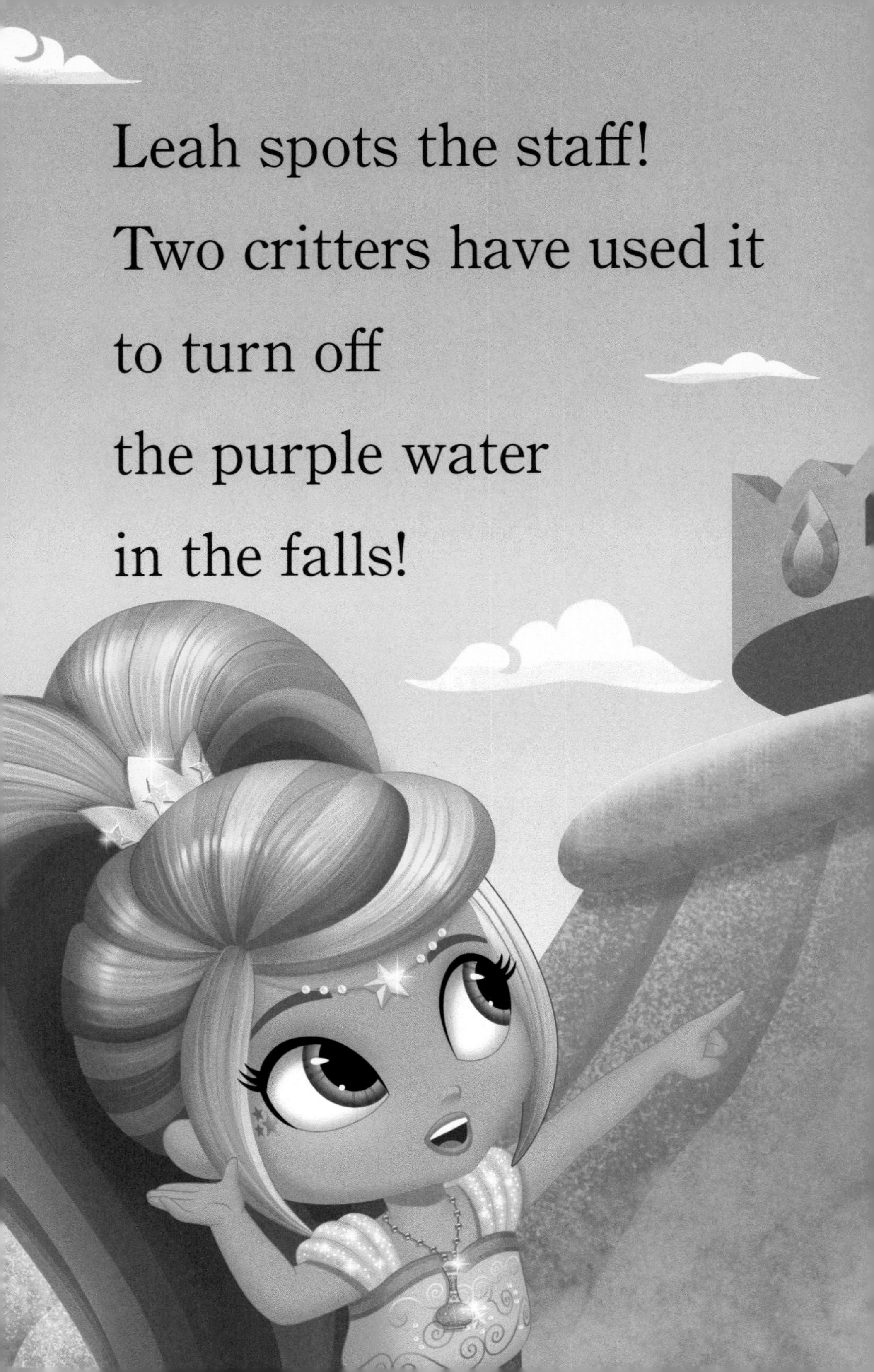

Leah spots the staff!
Two critters have used it
to turn off
the purple water
in the falls!

The critters
use the staff again
and turn off
the blue water.
A blue mist appears.

The blue mist makes shooting stars.

The friends run after the critters.

The critters turn
the green water
into a green mist.

The green mist makes
the ground bouncy!
The friends bounce
after the critters.

The critters turn
the red water
into a red mist.
The red mist brings
red chickens!

Then the critters
turn off the yellow
and the orange water.
Oops!
They break the staff!

All the water
from the rainbow falls
is trapped in
a giant genie bottle!

The friends must
open the bottle.
They bounce
to the top.

Working together, they push the stopper off the bottle.

All the colors
pour out!

Genie magic

works again!

Shimmer and Shine

fix Imma's staff.

The colors are back
in the rainbow falls,
and the genies can
fly again!

The genies and Leah
are glad they met Imma.
They are lucky
to have a new friend!